W9-BCO-480

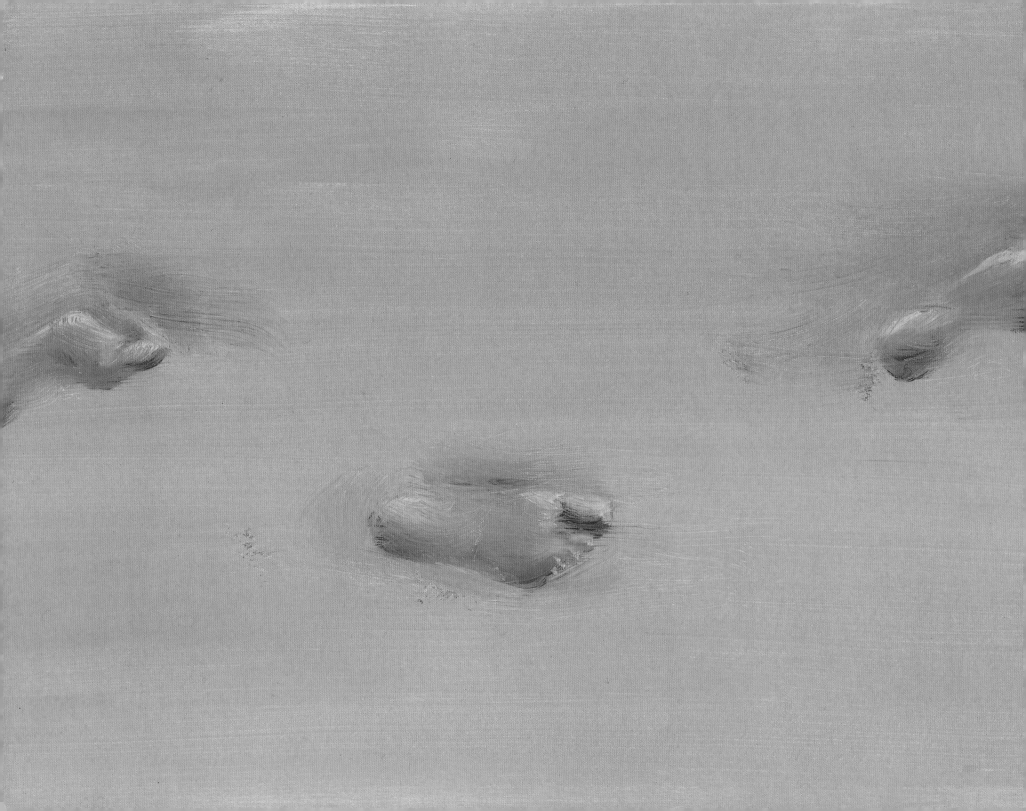

For Sam and Alice, who as brother and sister in the dawn of
the new millennium create greater light, imagination, and love
through their own sparkling storytelling—F. L.

To my wife, Michelle, and my son, Nelson. Thank you both
for the love and support you've given me—J. G.

2008 First U.S. edition
Text copyright © 2007 Frederick Lipp
Illustrations copyright © 2007 Jason Gaillard

Published by Charlesbridge
85 Main Street
Watertown, MA 02472
(617) 926-0329
www.charlesbridge.com

First published by Zero to Ten Limited
(a member of the Evans Publishing Group)
2A Portman Mansions, Chiltern Street,
London W1U 6NR, United Kingdom.
This edition published under license
from Zero to Ten Limited.

Library of Congress Cataloging-in-Publication Data
Lipp, Frederick.
    Running shoes / Frederick Lipp : illustrated by Jason
Gaillard.—1st U.S. ed.
       p. cm.
    Summary: Sophy, a determined young girl living in an
impoverished Cambodian village, fulfills her dream of going
to school—with the help of a pair of running shoes.
    ISBN 978-1-58089-175-2 (reinforced for library use)
    ISBN 978-1-58089-176-9 (softcover)
  [1. Education—Fiction. 2. Poor—Fiction. 3. Cambodia—
Fiction.] I. Gaillard, Jason, ill. II. Title.
PZ7.L6645Ru 2008
[E]—dc22   2007002285

Printed in China
(hc) 10 9 8 7 6 5 4 3 2 1
(sc) 10 9 8 7 6 5 4 3 2 1

Running Shoes

Frederick Lipp

Illustrated by Jason Gaillard

Charlesbridge

SOPHY LIVED IN A LAND where it was nearly always hot and sunny. When it finally rained, it rained for days and nights without end.

One terribly hot day, Sophy squinted her eyes against the blinding sun. The air was still. Suddenly a noise like bees swarming from a tree grew louder and louder. The pig began snorting. The chickens cackled.

Sophy sat up straight like a bamboo shoot. "Must be the number man's jeep," she thought as she rubbed her eyes.

Once a year a man came from the city in a red jeep. The village people called him the number man. He counted the number of people in the village for the government.

After making the rounds, the number man stopped at Sophy's house. "How many people live here?" he asked.

"Two," Sophy answered. "My mother and I."

"Let's see, that comes to one hundred fifty-four people in the village. Last year there were . . ." The number man stopped. He had heard that Sophy's father had died because there was no doctor or hospital near the village.

Sophy stared at the man's shoes.

"Ah, you have never seen running shoes before?" the man asked.

Sophy blushed. She thought about her secret wish. Her wish felt far, far away like a hawk lazily soaring in circles in the sky. Deep in her heart she knew her wish would come true if she had a pair of shoes like the number man's.

"Walk with me to the river," the number man said.

"Stick your feet into the clay. . . . Now step out." Sophy liked the warm feeling of mud squishing between her toes.

The number man took a stick with lots of numbers from his pocket. He measured Sophy's footprints.

Then the number man rubbed his chin as he mumbled numbers to himself. "Let's see. . . . In about a month, you will receive a surprise."

Sophy counted the days until a postal van drove through the village and dropped off a package by her door. She held her breath as she tore open the package.

"Running shoes!" she yelled. She carefully put on each shoe. "Now my wish will come true."

"What wish?" her mother asked.

"I want to go to school."

"But the school is eight kilometers away over horrible roads."

"Yes, but now I have running shoes!" Sophy said as she bounced up and down.

A smile slowly came over her mother's face. She remembered how Sophy's father sat with Sophy in the shade of a coconut tree and wrote marks on a small blackboard. He called them words. "This word is your name, Sophy, and this is the name of our village," he explained.

"You may go to school," Sophy's mother said.

The next day before the sun rose, Sophy ate a bowl of rice and a little salt fish. Then she set off through the rice fields, running.

The shoes protected her feet from the sharp, red rocks. She sailed through the air like a skipping stone over water.

Jumping over little streams, Sophy ran through the jungle on a narrow, winding road. She ran faster and faster until finally she saw the one-room schoolhouse.

Children's sandals were lined up outside the door.

Sophy hurriedly untied her running shoes, placed them by the
door, and walked barefoot into the schoolroom.

"My name is Sophy. I want to learn how to read and write."

The class, all boys, giggled.

"Quiet," the teacher said. "Come, you are welcome here. Where did you come from?"

"Andong Kralong."

The teacher gasped. "That is eight kilometers away!"

"Yes, Miss, but I have running shoes!"

The boys covered their teeth as they laughed. Tears rose
in Sophy's eyes. "I want to learn how to read."

"But you're a girl," one boy whispered.

Sophy pulled all her courage together like a green snake
ready to strike. She waited for the right time to speak.

After school Sophy tied on her running shoes with three knots in each shoe. She looked over the boys and said, "If you think you are so smart, try to catch me."

Boys pushed and shoved each other out of the way.

They ran after Sophy. No one could catch her.

The next morning, Sophy woke before the rooster's first call. Her head start allowed her to arrive at school before there were any sandals lined up at the door. When the boys paraded into the classroom, they smiled shyly.

They remembered how Sophy had won the race.

From that day on Sophy learned many subjects taught at the one-room schoolhouse.

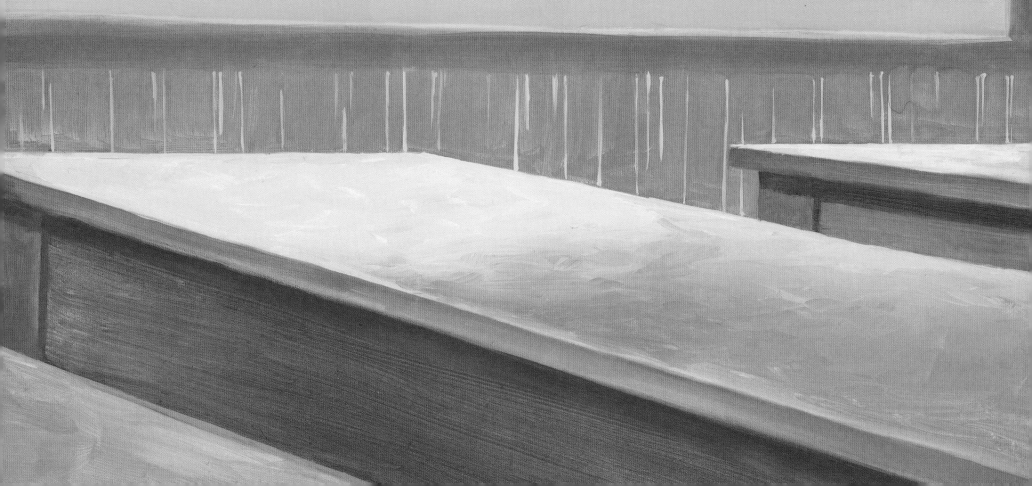

One morning a year later, Sophy was sitting with her mother when they saw a cloud of dust suddenly rise over the hill.

The pig began snorting. The chickens cackled.

It was the number man coming in his red jeep.

In that moment the first sprinkle of rain made little circles in the river. The circles grew larger. Monsoon was beginning.

Sophy looked up at the gathering clouds and thought she would be cooler in her daily race to school.

The number man counted everyone in the village.
At the end of the day he arrived at Sophy's house.

The number man looked down at Sophy's bare feet.

"Where are your running shoes?" he asked.

Sophy smiled and put her hands on her hips. "I only wear my running shoes when I go to school," she said.

They both laughed.

"I have something for you this time," Sophy said. "Follow me."

They walked to the side of the river. Sophy held a
bamboo stick and scratched words into the clay:

Thank you for the running shoes.
Now I can read and write.

Everything was so quiet that Sophy could hear the stream
bubbling around the stones. She looked down and said shyly,
"One day I want to help my people build a school and . . ."
"What?" the number man asked.
"I want to be the teacher," Sophy said, smiling and
wiggling her toes in the mud.

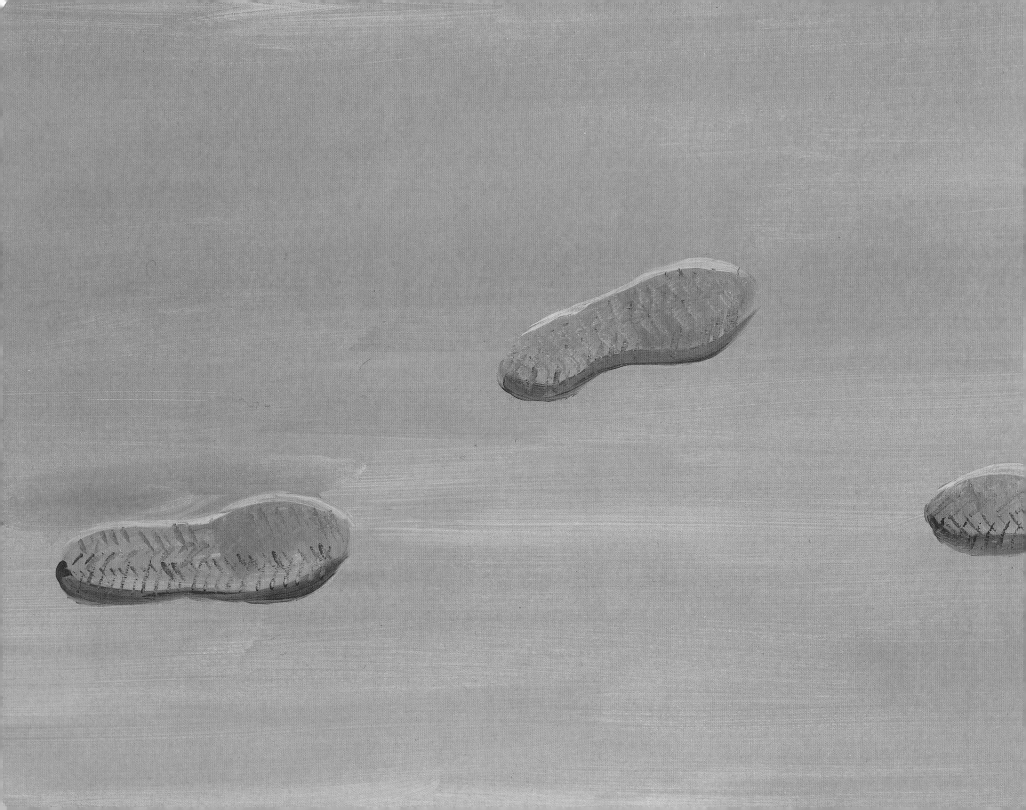

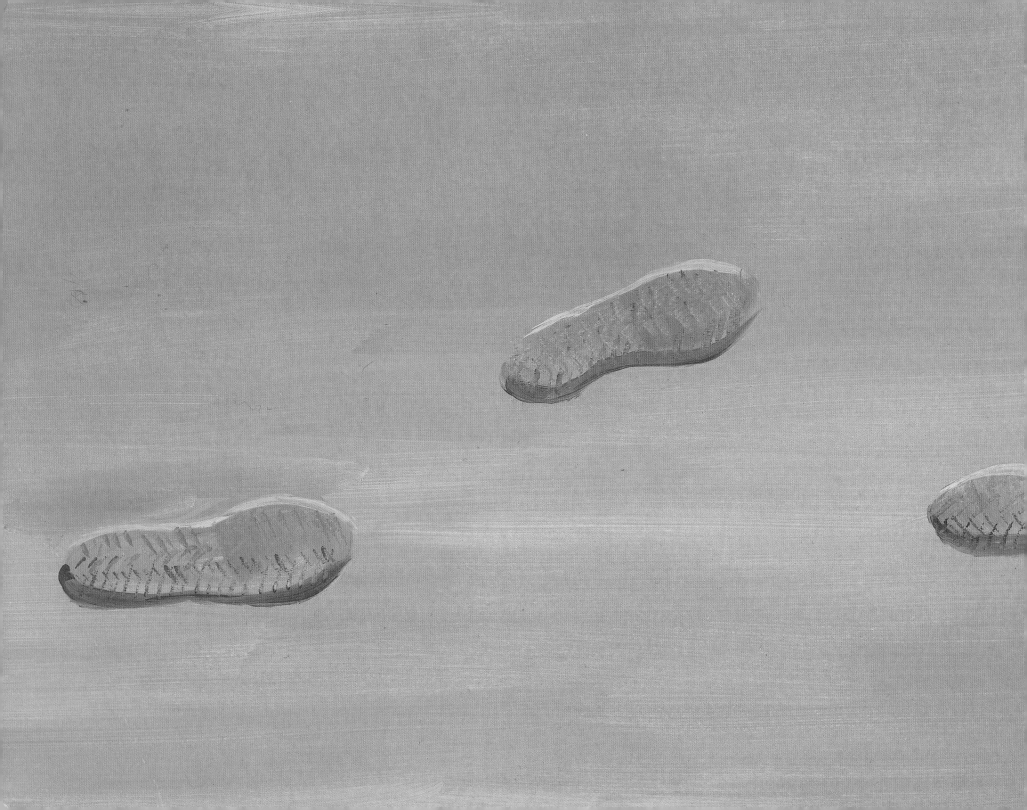